Where Is the Sears Tower?

WRITTEN BY TAD MITCHELL

ILLUSTRATED BY FRANCE MITCHELL

Thank you to France who painted tirelessly for years to make this a reality and whose eye for detail made all the difference in the text; to all my friends and family who provided encouragement, ideas, and edits; to Tricia, my editor; and to Douglas for doing the layout.

T.M.

Thank you to my loving husband who suggested this project as a venue to develop and share my talents and who believed in me and supported me through the many years; to my children who made do while I painted; to all my friends for their encouragement; and to God whom I leaned on for daily strength and comfort.

F.M.

First Printing

Printed in U.S.A.

Hardcover:
ISBN 13: 978-0-61547-828-9
ISBN 10: 0-61547-828-X

Softcover:
ISBN 13: 978-0-61547-318-5
ISBN 10: 0-61547-318-0

To order artwork visit: www.whereisthesearstower.com

For our children, Tamara, Taft, Tyler, and Truman.
May you always follow your inner compass.

University of Notre Dame

"I can't wait to see Grandpa," announced Peter as he anxiously fluttered from branch to branch. Peter and his mother lived at the University of Notre Dame in Indiana. She promised that he could visit his grandfather in Chicago when he turned one. Today was Peter's first birthday. The sun was rising, and Peter was ready to go.

"Come here, Peter," called his mother, "and stand still while I tell you how to get there." Peter landed next to his mother. "Fly to the great lake and then follow the shoreline west until you see the large buildings of Chicago. Once you are there, ask where the Sears Tower is. That is where Grandpa lives."

"That's easy, Mom. I know I can do it." Peter fluttered off again. "Can I go now?"

"Not yet. Come here, and pay attention. I have one more thing to tell you." Peter landed again. "Every time I left home, your grandfather would tell me, 'Remember your inner compass.'"

"I always do," replied Peter. "I don't even think about it. My compass tells me which way to fly when it's foggy or dark. I can even fly with my eyes closed."

Peter's mother smiled. "That compass is very important, but I am talking about *another* compass."

"Two compasses? That's silly. You mean one compass tells me to fly one way and the other compass tells me to fly another way?"

Peter's mother laughed. "Grandpa was talking about a different kind of compass–a feeling in your heart that helps you decide what to do and fills you with peace once you have made the right choice."

"Like the time those boys were being mean to Patty and I stood up for her? I was afraid they would be mean to me too, but something told me I should help her anyway. When they were hurtful to me, it didn't seem to matter after all, because helping her made me feel so warm inside."

"Exactly. You are so smart, Peter. When you go out into the world, you will meet all sorts of animals with all sorts of ideas about what you should do. Sometimes it will be confusing. It will feel like you are flying in the fog or the dark. You will need your inner compass to help you make the right choices."

"So if I am ever confused about what I should do, all I need to do is to listen to my inner compass," confirmed Peter.

"Precisely, and when you make the right choice you will feel good inside." She rubbed her cheek against his and whispered, "I love you, Peter."

"I love you, too, Mom. Can I go now?"

Peter's mother smiled. "Yes, you may go. Be careful. Have a nice visit with Grandpa, and give him a big hug for me."

Peter yelled, "Yippee!" as he dove off the branch. He circled around and waved to his mother and said, "Thank you so much for letting me go, Mom. I love you! Goodbye!"

"I love you, too! Goodbye, Peter!" she called, and then she sighed, "I will miss you so much." As she watched him fly away, a tear rolled down her cheek.

Soldier Field

Peter flew all morning. Finally, he noticed large buildings and a stadium ahead. He could hardly wait to see his grandfather. He spotted what he thought was a cat walking along a wall and decided to ask directions to the Sears Tower.

"Excuse me, Mr...." began Peter.

"Halt!" ordered the animal, whose tail popped up revealing he was a skunk, not a cat.

Peter froze.

The skunk peered into Peter's eyes, and demanded, "Who do you think you are? You do not have clearance to fly in my airspace, you do not have clearance to land here, and you did not address me as 'Sir.' I am Major Stink, the commanding officer of this sector. Son, don't you know how to follow protocol?"

Peter trembled. His feathers shook. He was afraid Major Stink might hurt him. Instinctively he was about to fly away when he had the thought that he was in no real danger. He realized he could fly away in an instant, and it was impossible for Major Stink to follow him. Peter's fear dissipated and confidence filled him. He challenged Major Stink. "Sir, how can this be your airspace if you cannot even fly?"

Major Stink became visibly upset and shouted, "I am the commander of this sector! No one questions me! What I say goes! When I talk, people listen! If I say the airspace is mine, it's mine!"

The shouting frightened Peter again, but he quickly remembered he had nothing to fear. Peter proceeded more judiciously this time. "Sir, since you are in charge of this sector, you must know the location of the Sears Tower."

Major Stink regained his composure. He liked that Peter had recognized that he was in charge. "Of course, I know the coordinates of the Sears Tower," he paused briefly and added, "but that is classified information."

Not thinking, Peter challenged Major Stink again. "Why is the location of the Sears Tower classified information?"

Major Stink lost his temper again. "It is classified because I say it is classified!"

Still at peace and no longer afraid, Peter realized he needed to be more careful with Major Stink.

Major Stink proceeded, "Boy, do you see that stadium? What's written on it?"

Peter read, "Soldier Field."

"You need to be a better soldier," commanded Major Stink. "You need to be brave and listen to orders."

"Yes, Sir," acknowledged Peter. Aware that Major Stink was not going to help him find the Sears Tower and anxious to get on with his trip, he politely excused himself. "Thank you, Sir. I need to get going now." Then Peter flew away.

Startled by Peter's sudden departure, Major Stink fired words at Peter as if he were trying to shoot him out of the sky. "This is my airspace! I told you! You do not have clearance! Land immediately!"

As Peter flew away, he marveled at the comforting peace that enveloped him, protecting him from the harsh words of Major Stink.

Shedd Aquarium

Peter continued flying along the lake looking for someone else to ask directions. He saw an owl perched in a tree. He was excited because he knew that owls were very wise. Certainly the owl would know the directions to the Sears Tower.

"Excuse me, Mr. Owl…" began Peter.

The owl cleared his throat. "*Professor* Owl."

"Excuse me, Professor Owl. Where is the Sears Tower?"

Professor Owl slowly turned his head toward Peter and spoke at a determined pace. "I love the Sears Tower. It is such a magnificent structure, an architectural marvel. Built between 1971 and 1973, the Sears Tower is the tallest building in the United States. It has 108 stories and stands 1,451 feet tall. With its antenna, it is 1,730 feet tall."

"Wow! That's very interesting. I can't wait to see it. I've come all the way from Notre Dame to visit…"

"Notre Dame!" exclaimed Professor Owl with delight. "I once did a study on dialects with Professor Mockingbird of Notre Dame. Have you read his book, *Say It Again*?"

"No," replied Peter. He flapped his wings and fidgeted on the branch. He was anxious to get going. He was about to give up on Professor Owl like he did with Major Stink. Then he had the feeling he should be patient and let Professor Owl speak his mind. Although Peter wanted to find his grandfather quickly, he knew in his heart that Professor Owl was only trying to help.

Peter tried again nicely, "Professor Owl, you are so wise that I'm sure you know where the Sears Tower is."

"Of course I do, but there is something you need to know first: there is no more Sears Tower."

"No more Sears Tower?" Peter gasped in disbelief. "How could it just disappear? Did they knock it down?" Peter worried about how he was going to find his grandfather now.

Professor Owl smiled. He finally had the young pigeon's undivided attention. "No, it did not disappear. They did not knock it down."

"So where is it then?" Peter was confused.

Professor Owl smiled broadly. He was very pleased that he had stumped Peter. "They renamed it. On July 16, 2009, at 10:00 AM Central Time, the Sears Tower was officially renamed the Willis Tower, but it will always be the Sears Tower to me."

"Willis Tower," Peter repeated slowly to make sure he had the name right. Then he returned to his original question, "So, where is the Willis Tower?"

Professor Owl straightened his feathers and cleared his throat. "The Willis Tower is between Jackson and Adams on Wacker." Professor Owl motioned toward the city with his left wing. "Did you know that all the East/West streets in that part of Chicago are named after United States presidents? There is Jackson, Adams, Madison, Monroe, Van Buren, and Harrison."

"Thank you for your help, Professor Owl. You are so wise. I'd like to stay longer, but I can't wait to see my grandfather at the Willis Tower, which was completed in 1973 and stands 1,730 feet tall." Peter winked.

"Class dismissed," announcer Professor Owl. "Come back sometime, and I will give you a tour of Chicago's Museum Campus. It has some of the best museums in the world–the Shedd Aquarium, the Alder Planetarium, and the Field Museum."

Buckingham Fountain

Peter gazed down, saw a beautiful fountain, and thought that he would stop for a drink. As he came in for a landing, he saw a rabbit on the grass nearby. He stopped short of the fountain to ask the rabbit directions. Now that he knew the correct name of the Sears Tower, he thought his search would go more quickly. "Excuse me, Mrs. Rabbit. Where is the Willis Tower?"

"Willis Tower!" Mrs. Rabbit panicked. "That's in the Loop. It's dangerous. You don't want to go there." She looked very concerned.

Peter looked around. "The Loop? Where is the Loop? I don't see any loops."

Mrs. Rabbit hopped closer to Peter and whispered, "The Loop is the business district of Chicago. It's called the Loop because there is a circular train line that loops around the area." Then she motioned toward the large buildings with her nose. "Technically Grant Park is in the Loop too, but it's not dangerous here."

Peter looked at the buildings with puzzlement. "Why is the Loop so dangerous?"

In a somber tone Mrs. Rabbit explained, "No rabbit that has gone into the Loop has ever returned." She bowed her head and looked as if she was going to cry. "My son, Hoppy, was too curious. He sneaked away into the Loop. He hasn't been seen since."

Peter bowed his head out of respect and said, "I'm sorry."

"Hoppy should have stayed here in Grant Park. There are 319 acres of safe parkland right along Lake Michigan, but he couldn't resist exploring the Loop," lamented Mrs. Rabbit.

Still, Peter was confused. Why would his grandfather live in such a dangerous place?

"When is the last time you heard from your grandfather?" questioned Mrs. Rabbit.

"It has been a while."

"I told you," declared Mrs. Rabbit. "It is dangerous. Stay away from the Loop. You won't come back."

Peter was perplexed. What Mrs. Rabbit was saying did not make sense. Was the Loop dangerous? Was his grandfather okay? He thought as hard as he could, but his mind was blank. Then, suddenly, everything became clear to him. He exclaimed with glee, "I figured it out! I know the truth now. The city is dangerous for rabbits since they can't fly, but the city is a great place for pigeons. There is plenty of food and many safe places to perch. In fact, it's more dangerous for me here than in the city."

"Listen here, young man," scolded Mrs. Rabbit. "If you want to live as long as I have, you had better mind your elders." Mrs. Rabbit hopped forward and looked Peter in the eyes. "Does your mother know you are here?"

"Of course she does. She sent me to Chicago to visit my grandfather at the Willis Tower."

"I can't believe it!" Mrs. Rabbit was visibly upset. She pulled a piece of grass and nervously chewed it until it vanished. "You stay here with me until we figure out what to do. We can't have a young pigeon like you roaming around the city all alone."

Just then there was a loud noise. Mrs. Rabbit froze. Without moving her mouth Mrs. Rabbit whispered, "Follow me," and she took off. She left so quickly that Peter had no idea where she went. After looking around for a while, he gave up. He fluttered over to the fountain, had a drink, and continued on his way.

Cloud Gate ("The Bean")

Peter continued flying over the park, coasting alongside the lake. Something bright caught his attention. It was a giant mirror in the shape of a bean. He had seen small reflective balls in flower gardens, but he had never seen one this large before. He landed on a nearby rose bush to admire it. As Peter was looking at the distorted buildings mirrored in the bean, he heard a voice.

"Hi, I'm Chuck. How do you do?" A groundhog appeared to Peter's left.

"Hi, I'm Peter. I'm fine. How are you?"

"Super duper!" chanted Chuck. "It's a great day to have some fun…and to eat! Every day's a great day for eating."

Peter chuckled. He thought Chuck was pretty funny.

"Chuck, do you know where the Willis Tower is?"

Instantly, Chuck replied in a serious tone, "Why? Did you lose it?" After a brief pause, he exploded in laughter. "Get it? Did you lose it?"

Peter laughed with him. Chuck seemed very pleased with himself.

"Try this," continued Chuck. Then as fast as he could he rattled, "How much wood would a woodchuck chuck if a woodchuck could chuck wood? A woodchuck would chuck all the wood he could chuck if a woodchuck could chuck wood!"

Peter laughed again. Then he tried, "How much wood would a wood…wood…could…I can't do it."

"It's not hard," encouraged Chuck. "You just have to practice. I practice all the time. Last year I won the Rapid Repeat Tongue-Twister Competition."

"Wow! You're good." Returning to his mission, Peter asked again, "Chuck, seriously, do you know where the Willis Tower is?"

"Yes, of course I do." Suddenly Chuck's eyes got very large. He looked distressed. His body went limp and he fell flat on his face. It looked as if he were dead.

Peter was shocked. He did not know what to do. He cried, "Chuck! Chuck! Are you okay?" Peter flew down from the rose bush next to Chuck's head and screamed again, "Chuck! Chuck! Are you okay?" Peter turned in circles, looking for help. He yelled, "Help! Help! Can someone help?"

After what seemed like forever, Chuck popped up on his hind legs, laughing hysterically. "I had you, didn't I?" Chuck had a huge smile on his face. "You thought I was dead, didn't you? That one gets everyone."

Peter was shaking from the shock of Chuck's mock death. At first Peter felt relieved. Then anger filled him. How could Chuck be so mean to scare him like that? His heart was still racing. His natural reaction was to want to peck Chuck. Turning away for a moment to try to calm down, Peter saw a rose in the bush. As he reflected on its beauty, he realized Chuck was a rose, not a thorn. Chuck did not mean to hurt Peter. He was just trying to make him laugh even though he had gone a bit too far. Peter's anger left him.

"I am pretty funny, aren't I?" gleamed Chuck.

"Yes, you are," smiled Peter. "Playing dead wasn't so funny for me, but otherwise you're very amusing. Thanks for making me laugh. I'm glad we met, but I need to get going now." As he flew away, Peter yelled, "Try this one: Peter Pigeon pecks perfect purple plums."

"That's pretty good. Keep practicing," Chuck shouted as he waved goodbye to Peter.

Chicago River

Peter decided to stop flying alongside the lake and to fly toward the buildings. He flew a couple of blocks and then was surprised when he saw a river, right in the middle of the city. He noticed a seagull perched on one of the river's bridges, and stopped to make sure he was heading in the right direction. "Excuse me, Mr. Seagull. Where is the Willis Tower?"

"Hello," cawed the seagull as he spread his wings. "I'm Sammy Seagull, the best fisherman in Chicago. How can I be of assistance to you?"

"I'm trying to find the Willis Tower."

"Willis Tower!" scoffed Sammy. "The fishing is no good by the Willis Tower. Let me tell you where you can find some good fishing holes. No one knows the Chicago River like Sammy."

"Thanks, but I don't know how to fish. I'm looking for my grandfather who lives at the Willis Tower."

"I *know* you don't know how to fish. Look at yourself. I used to be small like you. I started eating fish every day and look at me now. I'm almost twice as big as you."

Peter stood tall and puffed his chest. "I wish I were as big as you, but I can't fish because I can't swim."

Sammy shook his head. "I'm disappointed in you. With an attitude like that, you'll never learn to fish. Anyone who practices enough can be great like me. It's all about how hard you try."

"I wish I had webbed feet like yours. Then I could swim."

"That's a cop-out, son. You just need to paddle harder. If you try hard enough, you can do anything."

Peter was jealous. He wanted to be big like Sammy. He wanted webbed feet. Most of all, he wanted to be confident like Sammy. His friends would think he was so cool.

"How can I learn to fish?" asked Peter, fully believing in the impossible because he wanted so badly to be like Sammy.

"The first thing you need to learn is your approach. Let's fly down the river and practice by the Willis Tower. The fishing is not good there, so no one will be in our way." Sammy yelled, "Geronimo!" and dived straight down.

There were dozens of seagulls in the air, flying in every direction. Peter lost track of which one was Sammy. At least he had learned that the river led to the Willis Tower, except he did not know which way to follow it—left or right.

Peter decided to fly to his left. As he soared along the river with renewed hope, it occurred to him that wanting to be a seagull was silly. He would not grow bigger just because he ate fish. Paddling harder would not make him a swimmer. He was a pigeon, and being a pigeon was great. This thought brought peace to his mind. He realized that the peace had come from his inner compass. As he reflected, he also realized it was his inner compass that had told him not to fear Major Stink, to be patient with Professor Owl, and not to be angry with Chuck. Filled with warmth, he was determined that he would always listen to his inner compass.

Navy Pier

Before too long the river emptied into the great lake. He was disappointed, thinking that he must have flown past the Willis Tower. Just as Peter was about to shift his wings and turn around, he saw an egret standing on a breakwater in the middle of the lake. Peter landed next to the egret to ask directions. "Excuse me, Mrs. Egret. Where is the Willis Tower?"

"It's Ensign Egret. Can you wait a minute? I'm in the middle of something." Her neck snapped to various positions along the horizon.

Peter watched her for a minute and then asked, "What are you doing, Ensign?"

She continued surveying the horizon. After what seemed like a long time, she looked down at Peter. "Please, do not interrupt me. What I do is very important. I am responsible for the Navy Pier watch. I don't have much time. Please, be brief with your question."

"I am looking for my grandfather who lives…"

"One moment, please." Ensign Egret redirected her attention to a seagull cawing in the distance. "This is very important. Captain Seagull is relaying a critical message."

Peter waited for the seagull to stop cawing. "What did he say?"

"He said the wind is south by southwest at five knots."

"Why is that important?" asked Peter.

"I need to know everything that goes on at Navy Pier," she explained.

"What do you do with all the information?"

Ensign Egret was irritated. "I do not *do* anything with the information. I just *gather* it." She looked down at Peter. "I am very busy right now. Can we make an appointment for me to help you another time? Does next Tuesday work for you?"

Peter was discouraged and sad. He thought for sure he would find the Willis Tower with Sammy's instructions. Now he was perched on a breakwater in the middle of the lake far from any buildings, and Ensign Egret was too busy to help him. Tears welled up in his eyes. He did not know what to do. He felt like giving up. Just then, the sun shone brighter. It reminded Peter of what his mother often told him, "When a door shuts, a window opens." The thought filled him with hope. He was going to go find the window.

Peter apologized, "I'm sorry, Ensign. I guess I'll have to ask someone else."

"You could ask someone else, but you won't get as good of an answer. No one knows as much as I do." She resumed snapping her neck to various positions along the horizon as if Peter was not there.

Preparing to leave, Peter turned toward the city. "Wow! The city is so beautiful from here. I wish I could stay and enjoy the lake, but I need to find my grandfather before evening."

Ensign Egret was so busy that she did not even acknowledge what Peter had said. Peter flew back toward the city, admiring the magnificent skyline against the azure lake and feeling the warmth of the sun on his wings. He knew he would find his grandfather. He just needed to be patient and keep trying.

Ohio Street Beach

Peter neared the shore and saw a turtle sunning on the beach below. He decided to land and ask for directions. As Peter settled on the sand and tucked away his wings he cheerfully blurted, "Excuse me, Mr. Turtle. Where is the Willis Tower?"

Startled, Mr. Turtle yanked his head inside his shell. After a moment, he slowly peeked out, checked his surroundings, and peered nastily at Peter. "You are a cruel little pigeon. Why did you sneak up on me like that? That hurt my neck."

Peter was disturbed that Mr. Turtle had called him cruel. No one had ever called him that. He knew he was not cruel and was determined to show Mr. Turtle how nice he could be. "I'm sorry, Mr. Turtle. I didn't mean to hurt your neck."

Mr. Turtle looked away as if he had not heard Peter. Frustration filled Peter. He could not believe Mr. Turtle had ignored his nice apology.

All of a sudden, a wave rushed up the beach. Mr. Turtle moaned, "Not now!" Peter looked around trying to see what the matter was. "The waves are getting bigger. I just started my sunbath. Now I have to move up the beach. Nothing's ever easy."

Hoping to mollify the grumpy turtle, Peter commented, "It's a beautiful day for a sunbath."

"Sure it's a beautiful day for a sunbath," countered Mr. Turtle, shaking his head slowly back and forth, "but I have to walk all the way up the beach to get a good spot. Do you know how hard it is for a turtle to walk on sand? My feet slip. Sometimes my shell gets high centered, and I can't even move. Now that I'm old, I can only walk so fast."

Trying to help, Peter asked, "If it's that much work, why bother to take a sunbath?"

"Not take a sunbath? That's absurd," protested Mr. Turtle. "You are ignorant." Mr. Turtle ambled away from Peter, grumbling as he went, "I have to take a sunbath. That is what makes me happy."

Peter did not like being called cruel and ignorant. He was trying to be nice to Mr. Turtle, but it did not seem to matter. He was ready to give up and fly away. Then the thought came to him that he should not be offended by Mr. Turtle, and that Mr. Turtle was probably grumpy with everyone. Peter's frustration subsided, his mind cleared, and his focus returned to finding his grandfather.

Peter caught up with Mr. Turtle. "Do you know where the Willis Tower is? My mother sent me all the way from Indiana to visit my grandfather who lives at the Willis Tower."

Mr. Turtle continued walking away. Without looking back, Mr. Turtle sneered, "Your mother is a fool. She never should have sent you here. The city is huge. You will never find your grandfather."

Mr. Turtle had crossed the line by criticizing Peter's mother. He fumed, "Nobody speaks badly about my mother." He was so mad he flapped his wings and pecked Mr. Turtle's shell. Even though Peter remembered his mother scolding him for pecking others, he did not care. He pecked and pecked and pecked. Finally, with tears in his eyes, Peter took to the air. A somber feeling weighed Peter down as he drifted through the air. He felt sad, lost, and alone. He did not know which way to fly. He felt like giving up.

Magnificent Mile

Peter flew mindlessly up the shoreline, unsettled about pecking Mr. Turtle. Deep down he knew he should not have pecked him, but Mr. Turtle had insulted his mother. He told himself that he had made the right choice but did not understand why his heart was still heavy. Suddenly he realized that the tall buildings were ending, and he remembered that he needed to find the Willis Tower. He saw a beautiful city dog walking by the lake and thought he would ask for directions. Peter was sure that a city dog would know where the Willis Tower was.

"Excuse me, Miss Dog..."

"Please call me 'Princess.' 'Miss Dog' is so formal."

"Princess, where is the Willis Tower? My grandfather lives there and I am going to visit him."

"The Willis Tower? Oh, you mean the Sears Tower. Have they converted part of the Sears Tower into condos? What floor does your grandfather live on? I live on the 60th floor, lakeside view, by the Magnificent Mile."

"My grandfather lives on the top."

"Wow," gasped Princess. "That must be one expensive condo, but I still prefer living by the Magnificent Mile."

"What's the Magnificent Mile?"

"It's over there," Princess motioned with her nose. "It is a mile of Michigan Avenue with some of the best shopping in the world. I got my collar there. How do you like it?" Princess raised her head so Peter could admire it. "This is my casual collar. I have another one in pink that I wear when I go shopping."

Peter examined the green leather and shiny studs. "I have never seen anything so beautiful. It makes you look very sophisticated."

"Thank you." Princess lowered her head and blushed. After a brief pause Princess suggested, "You should really get something to dress yourself up, maybe an ankle bracelet. You are a good-looking pigeon. The ankle bracelet will make you look like a rock star."

"Do you really think so?"

"It definitely would. I would go with gold. It will sparkle as you fly."

Peter imagined himself wearing a gold ankle bracelet.

"Where can I get one?" asked Peter.

"There are lots of jewelry stores on the Magnificent Mile. My favorite is..."

Peter's mind wandered as Princess continued to talk. His mother was the most beautiful person he knew because of who she was, not because of what she looked like or what she wore. The ankle bracelet faded from his mind and his focus returned to finding his grandfather.

When Princess finished, Peter asked, "Is the Sears Tower by the Magnificent Mile?"

"No, but the Magnificent Mile is on the way to the Sears Tower. There are great restaurants there too. If you are not in the mood to go shopping, you should at least stop and have something to eat."

"Thank you for your help, Princess," said Peter. "I can't wait to see the Magnificent Mile."

Art Institute of Chicago

Peter flew straight into the city down Michigan Avenue. Princess was right. Peter had never seen so many stores and cars and people. There was so much to see that Peter lost track of time. Before he knew it, there were no more stores. The Magnificent Mile had ended. He knew he must be closer to his destination, and he needed to ask for directions again. He saw a squirrel by a lion statue and landed to ask him directions. He decided to try calling it the Sears Tower again. "Excuse me, Mr. Squirrel. Where is the Sears Tower?"

"Watch out," warned Mr. Squirrel as he darted behind the lion. "They're watching us."

Peter looked around and did not see anything. Confused, he turned to Mr. Squirrel and asked, "Who is watching us?"

Mr. Squirrel leaned close and whispered into Peter's ear, "The people. They come here all day long. They stop and stare. They want to capture me and force me to show them where my nuts are."

Peter wanted to laugh. Maybe he had misunderstood Mr. Squirrel. He repeated what Mr. Squirrel had said to confirm. "The people want to capture you, so they can steal your nuts?" Mr. Squirrel nodded as Peter spoke. Peter could not help himself. He chuckled, "That is the funniest thing I have ever heard."

Mr. Squirrel became very serious, and Peter forced himself to stop laughing. "That's fine if you want to ignore the dangers of the world, young man, but I don't take chances." Mr. Squirrel scanned his surroundings to make sure all the people were at a safe distance. Then he looked at Peter and suggested, "You may want to move closer to the statue."

"What?"

"You may want to move closer to the statue. Do you see that big oak branch above us?" They both looked up. "Oak branches are heavy and can crack right off without warning. That's why I stay close to the statue. That way I can always run under the statue for protection if it falls."

Peter smiled. The tree branch falling was just as ridiculous as the people stealing Mr. Squirrel's nuts.

A big breeze rustled the leaves in the tree, and Mr. Squirrel dived under the lion statue for protection. He beckoned to Peter, "Quick, get under here! The branch might break!"

Peter burst out laughing. Mr. Squirrel didn't appreciate Peter laughing at him. He shook his head in disgust and scurried off into the trees.

Peter's mistake hit him like a brick wall, and he got a sick feeling in his stomach. He did not mean to hurt Mr. Squirrel's feelings. He had laughed without thinking, and in doing so he had accidentally mocked Mr. Squirrel. He felt awful, just like he had when he pecked Mr. Turtle. Suddenly it became clear that he had made the wrong choice in pecking Mr. Turtle. He knew he needed to apologize this time. He flew from place to place looking for Mr. Squirrel and shouted, "Mr. Squirrel! Mr. Squirrel! I'm sorry. Where are you? I'm sorry." His cries became more and more desperate until all he could do was sob. It was too late. He had missed his opportunity to apologize.

As Peter sat there crying, he heard Mr. Squirrel's voice from behind him, "It's okay. A lot of people think I'm overly cautious." As Peter turned around, a breeze rustled the leaves again and Mr. Squirrel darted for cover.

Peter sniffled, "Thank you," and resolved within himself to always respect others.

The 'L'

Peter carefully navigated through the tall buildings. It was much more confusing than flying down Michigan Avenue. There was a train track that went over the road and blocked his line of vision. He thought that must be the train Mrs. Rabbit had told him about. He stopped atop a streetlamp to get his bearings and was surprised to find a chipmunk crouched in the beautiful flower basket that hung from it. Peter knew he had to be close to the Sears Tower. He just needed someone to point him down the right street.

"Hello, Mr. Chipmunk. Where is the Sears Tower?"

"Call me Chip. What's your name?"

"Peter."

Looking back and forth between Peter and the sidewalk, Chip wheedled, "Peter, you look like a very strong pigeon. I bet you can carry a lot. In fact, I bet you could easily get that bun on the sidewalk for me."

Peter knew helping Chip was the right thing to do, but he was anxious to see his grandfather, so he pushed the thought out of his mind. "That would be easy, but I'm in a hurry. I think I'm almost there. Please just point me toward the Sears Tower."

Chip shook his head. "I guess I was wrong. The bun must be too heavy for you."

Peter turned around on his perch in frustration. Peter thought that Chip must be very lazy or he would get the bun himself. "The bun is not heavy at all. It's just that I've come all the way from Notre Dame to visit my grandfather..."

"Then I am even more shocked. You come from a religious school, yet you do not take pity on a poor chipmunk." Chip frowned and turned away from Peter.

Peter turned away from Chip as well. He looked around trying to decide which way to fly next. Chip did not know what kind of a pigeon Peter was. The thought to help Chip briefly returned, but Peter pushed it out of his mind again and prepared to find someone else to give him directions.

"Don't you know your etiquette?" challenged Chip. "You visit my burrow, and you don't even bring me a house gift. Who taught you manners, young man?"

Peter ruffled his feathers. His mother had taught him manners. He was being polite to Chip. Chip was the one being rude, not him.

About to fly away, the thought to help Chip returned yet again. Instead of pushing it out of his mind this time, he listened to it. He dived down to the bun, picked it up, flew back up to the flower basket, and gave it to Chip. His bad thoughts about Chip faded. A huge burden was lifted from his mind. Warmth filled him. He realized that when he followed his inner compass he felt at peace with himself, and that when he resisted his inner compass he felt the need to justify his actions. He realized how much easier it was to follow his inner compass than to resist it, even if it was more work sometimes.

With a mouthful of bread, Chip looked up and said, "The Sears Tower is in the direction of the 'L.'"

"What's the 'L'?"

"The 'L' is the train. It's short for 'elevated.'" Chip motioned with his nose. "It's that way."

As Peter flew toward the train, he yelled, "Enjoy your bread. Thanks for the help."

Flamingo

Peter winged and weaved through the buildings with ease. He sensed he was close now, so close that anyone would know where the Sears Tower was. He saw a butterfly sitting on a sign in a plaza and stopped to ask directions.

"Excuse me, Miss Butterfly. Where is the Sears Tower?"

"The Sears Tower?" echoed Miss Butterfly. "The Sears Tower is…" She paused to think. Tears appeared in her eyes and she erupted into sobs, "I don't know where the Sears Tower is." She sniffled, "My parents abandoned me at birth. I had no one to teach me the names of the buildings. I know where the Flamingo sculpture is and where the Blue Line is. Why didn't you ask me that?"

Peter had not expected such a dramatic response. He was at a loss for words. Miss Butterfly continued to cry. Peter attempted to console her. "It's all right. A lot of people don't know where the Sears Tower is."

Miss Butterfly's sadness turned to fury. "You don't think I'm smart," snapped Miss Butterfly. "You think that because I spent half my life inside a chrysalis that I don't know anything."

Peter was taken aback by how defensive she was. "I'm sure you're smart. I didn't mean to hurt your feelings. I'm just trying to find my grandfather who lives at the Sears Tower."

Miss Butterfly started laughing hysterically. "You are trying to find the Sears Tower, and you didn't bring a map?" Miss Butterfly doubled over laughing. "You silly pigeon, it's not my fault that you're unprepared."

Peter was becoming uncomfortable due to Miss Butterfly's sudden mood changes. He tried to dismiss himself. "It's okay. I can ask someone else," he said.

"Someone else?" whined Miss Butterfly. "You don't like me, do you? I'm doing the best I can."

Growing even more uneasy, Peter wondered if Miss Butterfly was in her right mind. Judgments filled his head: "She probably does not have many friends because she is so volatile. She probably has nothing better to do than sit on the sign and pester people all day."

Suddenly a thought hit Peter stronger than any other thought that day. He knew that even if Miss Butterfly was a little different, she was just as special, important, and loved as him–that they were equals. He knew the thought came from his inner compass and felt a tingling in his body.

The sun reflected off a glass building illuminating Miss Butterfly's wings. "Wow! Your wings are stunning!" proclaimed Peter.

Miss Butterfly motioned like she was going to counter what Peter just said, but she was dumbfounded.

Peter continued, "The colors are so vibrant. The designs are so intricate."

Miss Butterfly blushed, still speechless.

"I'm so glad we met. I've never seen a butterfly close up before." Peter waved as he prepared to take off. "Have a wonderful day. I need to go find the Willis Tower now."

"Wait!" burst out Miss Butterfly. "You said Sears Tower before, not Willis Tower. The Willis Tower is right over there." She motioned with her wing. "I fly by it every day. There's a huge 'Willis Tower' sign in front of it." Miss Butterfly radiated with delight.

Peter was speechless. "I'm so thankful I met you. You made my day!"

Willis Tower

Peter flew to the building Miss Butterfly had pointed at. He landed on a ledge by an outdoor dining area. Pigeons were happily pecking at food that had fallen to the ground. Peter gazed up at the Willis Tower. He was amazed by how tall it was. All of a sudden, out of nowhere, a pigeon landed on the ledge next to him. It was his grandfather!

"I've been watching for you all afternoon," welcomed Grandpa as he gave Peter a big hug.

"Here's a big hug from Mom. I'm so happy to see you, Grandpa. It was such a long trip."

"Yes. It is long trip from Notre Dame."

"No. Not that part. The long part was when I got to Chicago. It was so hard to find the Sears Tower. I had to ask eleven animals where it was before I found it. I also learned that it's now called the Willis Tower, not the Sears Tower."

"Oh," said Grandpa apologetically. "I forgot to mention that they changed the name. I still call it the Sears Tower. Lots of people do."

"That's okay. It was an adventure."

"An adventure," smiled Grandpa. "Did you use your inner compass on your adventure?"

Peter had a look of surprise. "How did you know Mom would tell me about the inner compass?"

Grandpa grinned.

Words gushed from Peter's mouth, "It's so cool. All I do is listen, and it helps me with everything."

Grandpa grinned wider. "What do you mean it helps you with everything?"

"It helped me with each animal I met along the way." Peter was so excited to share his experiences he could hardly talk fast enough.

"When I met Major Stink, it chased away my fears and filled me with peace."

"When I met Professor Owl, it helped me be patient."

"When I met Mrs. Rabbit, it showed me the truth."

"When I met Chuck, it melted away my anger and filled me with love."

"When I met Sammy Seagull, it helped me be happy with who I am."

"When I met Ensign Egret, it took away my sadness and filled me with hope."

"When I met Mr. Turtle, I learned that my inner compass leaves me when I do not listen to it."

"When I met Princess, it taught me that true beauty comes from within."

"When I met Mr. Squirrel, it reminded me that I should always show respect."

"When I met Chip, it helped me forget myself and be kind."

"When I met Miss Butterfly, it taught me that everyone is special in their own way."

Grandpa beamed. "I'm so pleased with you, Peter. Today you have learned how to listen to your inner compass—the only way to find true happiness. However, your lesson is not over. You need to practice every day."

"Every day?"

"Yes, Peter, every day. As you get older and wiser, you may start thinking you're smarter than your inner compass and stop listening. You need to remain teachable and keep listening to it. If you do, your inner compass will be a beacon on the horizon for you for the rest of your life and you will never be lost."

The End

Appendix

Map

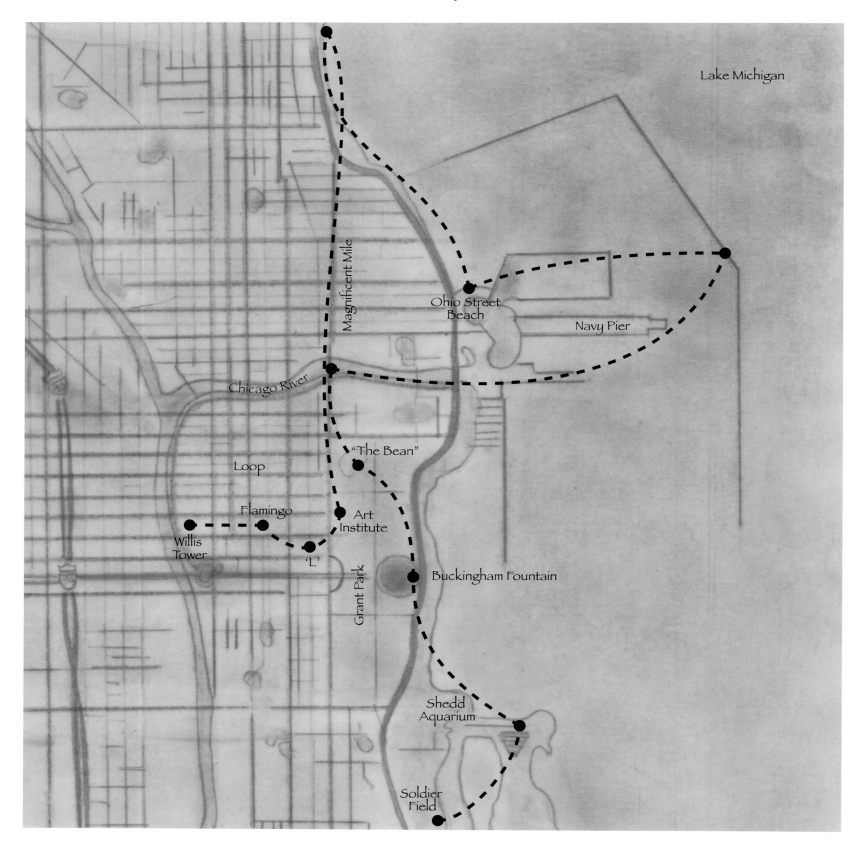

Lake Michigan

Magnificent Mile

Ohio Street Beach

Navy Pier

Chicago River

"The Bean"

Loop

Flamingo

Art Institute

Willis Tower

'L'

Grant Park

Buckingham Fountain

Shedd Aquarium

Soldier Field

Landmarks

University of Notre Dame

The University of Notre Dame du Lac (French for Our Lady of the Lake) is a private Catholic university located northeast of South Bend, Indiana and was founded in 1842. Its centerpiece is the Main Building, which is topped with a gold dome and a statue of St. Mary. The Main Building was destroyed by fire in the spring of 1879 and was speedily rebuilt by the fall semester of that same year. It is now home to Notre Dame's administration.

Soldier Field

Soldier Field is a memorial to American soldiers who have died at war. Officially opened on October 9, 1924, the 53rd anniversary of the Great Chicago Fire, the memorial's original name was Municipal Grant Park Stadium. On November 11, 1925 its name was changed to Soldier Field. In September 1971 it became the home of the Chicago Bears who previously played at Wrigley Field. It reopened on September 29, 2003 after its second complete rebuild.

Shedd Aquarium

The John G. Shedd Aquarium opened in 1930. It was the first inland aquarium with a permanent saltwater fish collection and is located on Museum Campus Chicago, which it shares with the Adler Planetarium and the Field Museum of Natural History. Gifted to the city by retailer John G. Shedd, the aquarium features a subterranean wild coral reef and a 400,000-gallon shark exhibit.

Buckingham Fountain

Buckingham Fountain, dedicated in 1927, is located in Grant Park. Donated to the city by Kate Buckingham in memory of her brother, Clarence Buckingham, the fountain represents Lake Michigan, with each seahorse symbolizing a state bordering the lake. The design of the fountain was based on the Bassin de Latome and was modeled after Latona Fountain at Versailles.

Cloud Gate ("The Bean")

Cloud Gate is a sculpture by Anish Kapoor and is located in Millennium Park. Inspired by liquid mercury, it is made of stainless steel plates welded together and then polished so the seams become invisible as it reflects the city's skyline. Constructed between 2004 and 2006, it stands 33 feet high by 66 feet long by 42 feet wide and weighs 110 short tons. It is nicknamed "The Bean" because of its bean-like shape.

Chicago River

The Chicago River runs through downtown Chicago and connects the Great Lakes with the Mississippi River, which is why Chicago became so important. Originally the river emptied into Lake Michigan, but in the 1800s civil engineers reversed its flow inland to keep the city's water supply (Lake Michigan) clean. The river is famous for the tradition of dyeing it green on St. Patrick's Day. Dozens of movable bridges cross the river and are opened to let sailboats travel to and from Lake Michigan.

Navy Pier

Navy Pier was first opened to the public in 1916 as "Municipal Pier #2." At the time, it was the largest pier in the world, designed for shipping and public gatherings. Used by the military in World War I and II, in 1927 it was officially named Navy Pier in honor of the Naval personnel who served there during World War I. Between 1946 and 1965 the pier was used by the University of Illinois as a location to educate returning veterans. In the 1990s, Navy Pier underwent a major renovation and is now Chicago's number one tourist attraction, featuring entertainment, shopping, dining, and events.

Ohio Street Beach

Ohio Street Beach is located in Olive Park just north of Ohio Street. It is one of dozens of beaches along the Lake Michigan shoreline. Facing north, rather than the usual east, Ohio Street Beach formed on its own in a bay created by the Jardine Water Purification Plant, which juts out into the Lake.

Magnificent Mile

The Magnificent Mile, also referred to as "The Mag Mile," is the portion of Michigan Avenue extending from the Chicago River north to Oak Street. Home to Chicago's largest shopping district, the Mag Mile includes popular sites such as the Drake Hotel, John Hancock Center, Wrigley Building, and Tribune Tower. It also features the Chicago Water Tower, the second-oldest water tower in the United States and the only downtown building that survived the Great Chicago Fire of 1871.

Art Institute of Chicago

The Art Institute of Chicago, located in Grant Park, is the second-largest art museum in the United States. The building was constructed for the World's Columbian Exposition in 1893 with the intent to use it for the Art Institute afterward. The Art Institute's Michigan Avenue entrance is guarded by two bronze lion statues. When Chicago professional sports teams play in championships, the lions are clothed in that team's uniform. The lions also wear wreaths around their necks during the holiday season.

The 'L'

The 'L' is the public rapid-transit system that services Chicago and its outlying suburbs. The oldest parts of the 'L' started operating in 1892 with wooden cars and a steam engine. The 'L' (from "elevated") is the third-busiest rail mass-transit system in the United States, and was voted by *Chicago Tribune* readers as one of the "seven wonders of Chicago."

Flamingo

Flamingo is a sculpture by Alexander Calder located in Federal Plaza in front of the Kluczynski Federal Building. It stands 53 feet high, weighs 50 tons, and is made of steel painted bright vermilion. The sculpture was unveiled on October 25, 1974, the same day as the unveiling of Calder's *Universe* motorized mobile in the lobby of the Sears Tower.

Willis Tower

The Willis Tower, formerly named the Sears Tower, is a 1,452-foot skyscraper completed in 1973. At the time, it was the tallest building in the world and remained so for 25 years. It still is the tallest building in the United States. Sears, Roebuck & Co., the largest retailer in the world at the time, constructed the building as a means of consolidating several of their smaller offices around the Chicago area. In March 2009 Willis Group Holdings, Ltd., a London-based insurance broker, leased a portion of the building and obtained the naming rights. On July 16, 2009, the building was officially renamed Willis Tower.

Animals/Insect

Rock Pigeon

Rock pigeons, or rock doves, live in cities, farmland, or rock cliffs; eat seeds and fruit; and are commonly found in flocks. Some of their predators are raccoons, opossums, owls, and eagles. Pigeons can find their way home even if released blindfolded from distant locations. Rock pigeons were used in World War I and II to carry messages. Rock pigeons have established their habitats in cities around the world.

Skunk

Skunks are known for their self-defense mechanism, a pungent and hard-to-remove spray that can travel as far as 10 feet. They are nocturnal foragers that eat mostly insects and small mammals but also eat grubs, birds' eggs, and fruit. Most skunks live in the Americas. They can dig their own burrows but will often use hollow logs, abandoned dens of other animals, or other convenient spaces. Most predators avoid skunks except for certain owls that do not seem to mind the smell.

Owl

Most owls hunt at night with their excellent hearing, night vision, and ability to fly silently. Their prey is typically small mammals like mice, squirrels, and rabbits. They swallow small prey whole since they have no teeth. If their prey is large, they rip it into pieces first with their strong claws and razor-sharp beaks. They later regurgitate pellets of indigestible materials like bones and fur. Owls cannot move their eyes in their sockets; rather they rotate their head up to 270 degrees. Owls are found on every continent except Antarctica.

Rabbit

Despite being on the menu of almost every predator, rabbits thrive because of their ability to reproduce. Rabbits can have three to four litters of four to five young (known as kittens) each year. Gestation is only about 30 days and rabbits can begin breeding as early as 3–4 months of age. Rabbits are the only animal that can produce 10 times their own weight in offspring in one year. Rabbits feed on leafy plants during the growing season and the buds and bark of woody plants in the winter.

Groundhog

Groundhogs, or woodchucks, gorge themselves in the summer to build reserves of fat and then retreat to their den to hibernate in the winter. Their hibernation gives rise to the American tradition of Groundhog Day. Folklore dictates that if the groundhog sees his shadow when he emerges from his hole, there will be six more weeks of winter. Groundhogs usually stay on the ground but can also climb trees and swim. They can also dig multi-entrance burrows up to five feet in depth.

Seagull

Seagulls are scavengers. They are often seen in large, noisy flocks congregating wherever food is available, usually by fishing boats, picnic grounds, and garbage dumps. Besides eating dead animals and organic litter, they also eat fish and crabs. Some are so aggressive that they will take food from humans. Many consider seagulls to be a nuisance, but they actually perform a very valuable service by removing garbage. Most seagulls live on the coast or inland and nest on the ground in colonies. Seagulls have a special pair of glands that allow them to drink salt water.

Egret

Egrets inhabit the eastern half of North America. At the beginning of the 20th century, they neared extinction because their feather plumes were in great demand for use in women's apparel. Even though egrets are now protected by law, their species is still threatened by the loss of wetlands where they nest in colonies. An adult egret's wingspan is almost five feet. They catch fish by standing motionless on their long legs in water. They also eat frogs, salamanders, snakes, crayfish, mice, and insects.

Turtle

Turtles are known for their hard, protective, camouflage shell, which is made of more than 50 bones connected together. When frightened, turtles retract their head, tail, and limbs into their shell until the threat is gone. Turtles are cold blooded and regulate their temperature by basking in the sun or sitting in a puddle, and hibernate in the winter. Instead of teeth, turtles have a sharp beak for eating plants and small creatures such as fish, worms, or crickets. Turtles lay their eggs on land. Several species of turtles can live to be more than a hundred years old.

Dog

Dogs were originally domesticated from wolves thousands of years ago and have evolved into hundreds of breeds. Dogs are highly social and trainable, allowing them to fit well into human households. Dogs and humans treat each other as members of their respective family, earning dogs their title as "man's best friend." Dogs can be trained to work, filling many roles in society, but their most popular role is that of a companion. Most dogs can detect smells and sounds much better than humans.

Squirrel

Squirrels nest in trees and return there each evening. During storms or severe cold they may stay in their nest for days, but squirrels do not hibernate. Squirrels normally live alone, but will temporarily share their nest if it is extremely cold. Squirrels eat nuts, seeds, and fruit. They hide their extra nuts and then hunt for them when they get hungry. A squirrel's bushy tail helps it balance, provides shade from the sun, gives warmth in the cold, and helps it communicate with other squirrels. A squirrel's front teeth grow six inches a year but are worn down from everyday use.

Chipmunk

Chipmunks dig two-inch–wide tunnels and make burrows in tunnel systems that can be up to 30 feet long and typically have several sleeping areas, food storage areas, and various entrances. When they dig their tunnels, chipmunks do not leave any dirt at the entrance. Instead they carry away the dirt in their cheeks so as not to attract predators. Chipmunks hibernate, waking every two weeks or so to eat. They can climb trees to harvest nuts but prefer to forage on the ground if possible. A chipmunk's mouth is small, but its cheeks can expand to three times its head size.

Butterfly

Butterflies begin as eggs that later hatch into larvae. The larvae grow rapidly, shedding their skin several times before arriving at their final skin, a pupa that hardens into a chrysalis. (Moths spin cocoons. Butterflies do not.) After about two weeks of metamorphosis, the adult butterfly emerges to drink nectar, mate, lay eggs, and die. Monarch butterflies migrate thousands of miles each year to California or Mexico and back. They breed along the way so the returning butterflies are several generations removed.